Sleep, Baby, Sleep

Maryann Cusimano Love

illustrated by Maria van Lieshout

PHILOMEL BOOKS ★ PENGUIN YOUNG READERS GROUP

PHILOMEL BOOKS

A division of Penguin Young Readers Group.
Published by The Penguin Group.
Penguin Group (USA) Inc., 375 Hudson Street, New York, NY 10014, U.S.A.
Penguin Group (Canada), 90 Eglinton Avenue East, Suite 700, Toronto, Ontario M4P 2Y3, Canada
(a division of Pearson Penguin Canada Inc.).
Penguin Books Ltd, 80 Strand, London WC2R 0RL, England.
Penguin Ireland, 25 St. Stephen's Green, Dublin 2, Ireland (a division of Penguin Books Ltd).
Penguin Group (Australia), 250 Camberwell Road, Camberwell, Victoria 3124, Australia
(a division of Pearson Australia Group Pty Ltd).
Penguin Books India Pvt Ltd, 11 Community Centre, Panchsheel Park, New Delhi - 110 017, India.
Penguin Group (NZ), 67 Apollo Drive, Rosedale, North Shore 0632, New Zealand
(a division of Pearson New Zealand Ltd).
Penguin Books (South Africa) (Pty) Ltd, 24 Sturdee Avenue, Rosebank, Johannesburg 2196, South Africa.
Penguin Books Ltd, Registered Offices: 80 Strand, London WC2R 0RL, England.

Published simultaneously in Canada. Manufactured in China by South China Printing Co. Ltd.

Design by Ryan Thomann. Text set in Latienne Medium.

Library of Congress Cataloging-in-Publication Data
Cusimano, Maryann K.   Sleep, baby, sleep / Maryann Cusimano Love ; illustrated by Maria van Lieshout.   p. cm.
Summary: As their baby sleeps, the parents wish for their child the many characteristics found in animals,
such as being gentle as a lamb, having the sight of a hawk, and the peacefulness of a snowy dove.
[1. Stories in rhyme. 2. Parent and child—Fiction. 3. Animals—Habits and behavior—Fiction.] I. Van Lieshout, Maria, ill. II. Title.
PZ8.3.C965Sl 2009   [E]—dc22   2008025750
ISBN 978-0-399-24753-8

3 5 7 9 10 8 6 4
Special Markets ISBN 978-0-399-25510-6
Not for Resale

To Ava Rose, Ricky, Maria, and Rich,
may your wishes come true. —M.C.L.

For Maia, Daan, Natalie, Alicia and Isa. —M.v.L.

Sleep, baby, sleep,
snuggled like a sheep.
Be always like the lamb so mild,
a kind and sweet and gentle child.
Sleep, baby, sleep.

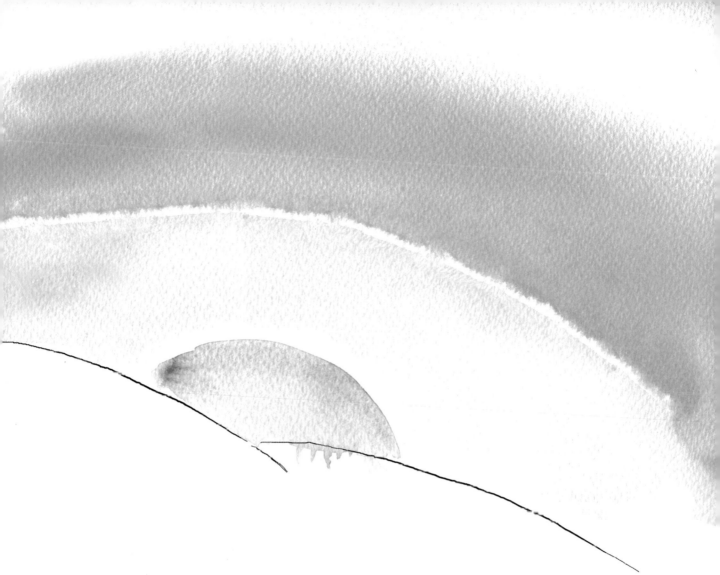

Rise, baby, rise.
Wipe the sleep from your eyes.
Be like the chick who leaves her shell
to toddle over field and dell.
Rise, baby, rise.

Soar, baby, soar.
The whole world you'll explore.
Fly like the goose who climbs and roams
yet always knows his way back home.
Soar, baby, soar.

Laugh, baby, laugh.
Frolic like the calf,
nose tickled by the grass and rye,
eyes twinkling at the beaming sky.
Laugh, baby, laugh.

Look, baby, look,
surprise in every nook.
Be like the hawk who trusts her sight
of canyons grand and feathers slight.
Look, baby, look.

Climb, baby, climb,
one step at a time.
Be like the cub who scales great trees
to peer above the canopy.
Climb, baby, climb.

Sail, baby, sail,
calm in the windy gale.
Be like the duck who paddles through
the storm to glide in waves of blue.
Sail, baby, sail.

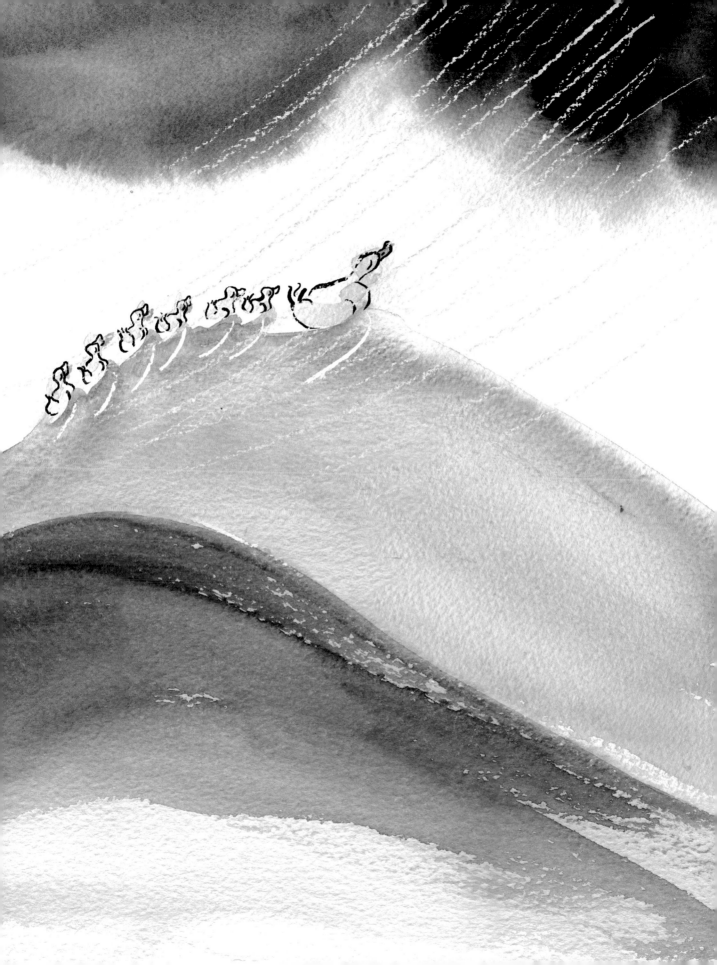

Splash, baby, splash.
Stand tall as the waves crash.
Be always like the hound who dares
to find adventure everywhere.
Splash, baby, splash.

Grow, baby, grow.
From our arms you'll go,
unfurling like a butterfly,
cocoon opening to the sky.
Grow, baby, grow.

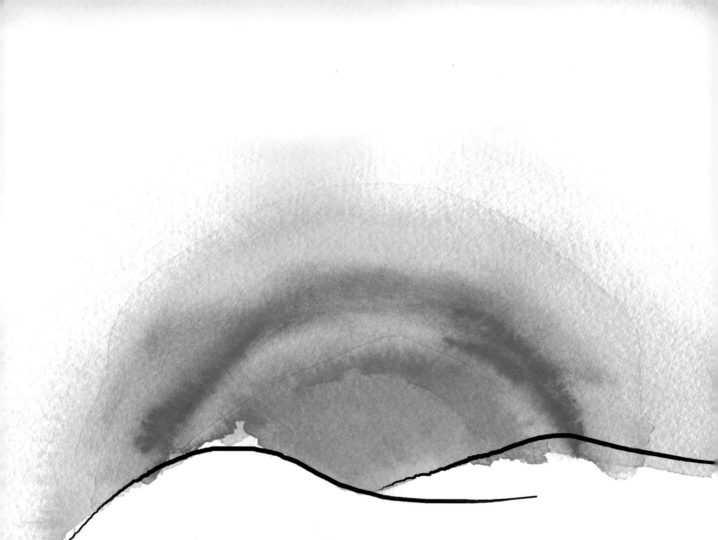

Hush, baby, hush.
Growing can't be rushed.
Be always like the newborn foal
with whispered wind songs in his soul.
Hush, baby, hush.

Shine, baby, shine,
graceful child of mine.
Be like the firefly who glows
no matter how the darkness grows.
Shine, baby, shine.

Peace, baby, peace.
All your cares release.
Be always like the snowy dove
who spreads her wings and sings of love.
Peace, baby, peace.

Dream, baby, dream,
rising like moonbeams.
Be always like the dragonfly
shimmering in the misty sky.
Dream, baby, dream.

Sleep, baby, sleep.

Our promises we'll keep.

Be the miracle you are,

a wish come true on a shooting star.

Sleep, baby, sleep.

Author's Note

It all began with Mother Goose.

Sleep, baby, sleep, down where the woodbines creep.
Be always like the lamb so mild, a kind and sweet and gentle child.
Sleep, baby, sleep.

Rocking our babies back to sleep in the wee hours, I began this lullaby with the soothing rhythm of the old Mother Goose rhyme, adding music to go with the verse. But I needed more verses to send our children to sleep, and I didn't want to celebrate children only for being meek as lambs. So *Sleep, Baby, Sleep* was born in the adaptive tradition of Mother Goose, moving beyond the original verse, encouraging children to soar and dream as beings of strength and courage. I hope your family enjoys sharing this lullaby as ours has.

—*Maryann Cusimano Love*